Pigmeleon
(pig-chameleon)

Skunkatoo
(skunk-cockatoo)

Rhumbler
(rhinoceros-beaver-bumble bee)

Vernalynda
(sheep-moose-shoebill)

Snog
(snail-warthog)

Hissypoo
(snake-poodle)

Flavian
(crocodile-ram-scorpion)

Nib
(piranha-mouse-spider)

Turducken
(turkey-duck-chicken)

Trixie Dillo
(giraffe-armadillo)

Figley vs. the Mookling Hat

Written by Suzanne Cotsakos & Ryan McCulloch

Illustrated by Ryan McCulloch

MUTASIA CHILDREN'S ENTERTAINMENT

For Robert and Brianna

WRITTEN BY:
Suzanne Cotsakos
Ryan McCulloch

ILLUSTRATED BY:
Ryan McCulloch

CREATIVE CONCEPTS BY:
Tami Cotsakos
Suzanne Cotsakos
Ryan McCulloch

SPECIAL THANKS:
Dr. Christos M. Cotsakos, Alex Kampmann, Brianna McCulloch, Julianne Miles,
Pauline Neuwirth, Liz Rodriguez, Brigitte VanBaelen

Published by Mutasian Entertainment, LLC

Printed in China

Discover Mutasia's books, music, stuffed animals, and more at mutasia.com

A portion of all profits go to organizations that benefit children.

Distributed by Midpoint Trade Books

ISBN: 978-0692106327
LCCN: 2018947209

First Edition

Figley vs. the Mookling Hat

Welcome to the island of **Mutasia**, where everyone is a mixed-up mix of two or more different animals.

Mutasia is filled with so many kooky combinations,
you'd have to see it to believe it!

This cute and cuddly critter is called a **mookling**. Mooklings are part duck and part moose. These antlered animals are very friendly.

A new fashion craze was
sweeping through the island
of Mutasia...

MOOKLING HATS!

It all started when Mutasia's queen tied
a mookling to her head. It didn't take
long before everyone else copied her
fabulous, feathery new look!

Chadwick had a
mookling hat.

Zabetta had a
mookling hat.

Billie Twinklecorn had a mookling hat and Julio Habañero had a mookling hat.

Rhumbler, Rufus, and Wattee each had a mookling hat.

Even Flavian, the grumpy old monster who lives in a cave, had a mookling hat.

Everyone on Mutasia had a mookling hat. Everyone,
that is, except Figley. Figley felt like he didn't fit in.

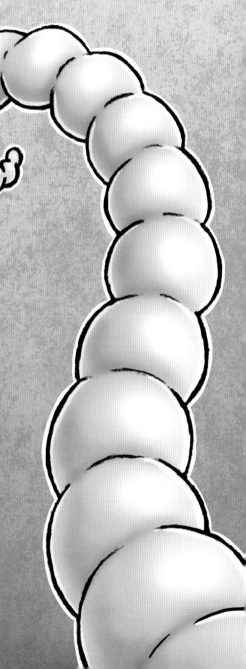

Tonight is the night of Billie Twinklecorn's **big party**.
Figley knew if he showed up looking different than
everyone else, he'd be a laughing stock!

He was going to need a mookling hat . . . fast! Unfortunately, all the stores were sold out. That meant he was going to have to catch a mookling himself.

But how?

Figley tried **everything!**

He tried to catch a mookling with his fishing pole and a slice of bread.

He tried to trap one using a trail of crumbs.

He even tried to woo one with a beautiful mookling sock puppet.

No luck.

After hours in the jungle, Figley finally had a mookling in his grasp! But this mookling was stubborn.

Figley tried to hold on to its webbed foot, but lost his grip. He fell face first into a swampy pond as the stubborn mookling flew away.

Figley was heartbroken.
There was no way he would
have a mookling hat before
the party started.

Suddenly, a silly, squishy face
appeared in the water . . .

. . . and Figley had
an interesting idea

Later that evening, at Billie's party, the sounds of dance music and quacking filled the air! **Everyone** was wearing a mookling hat . . .

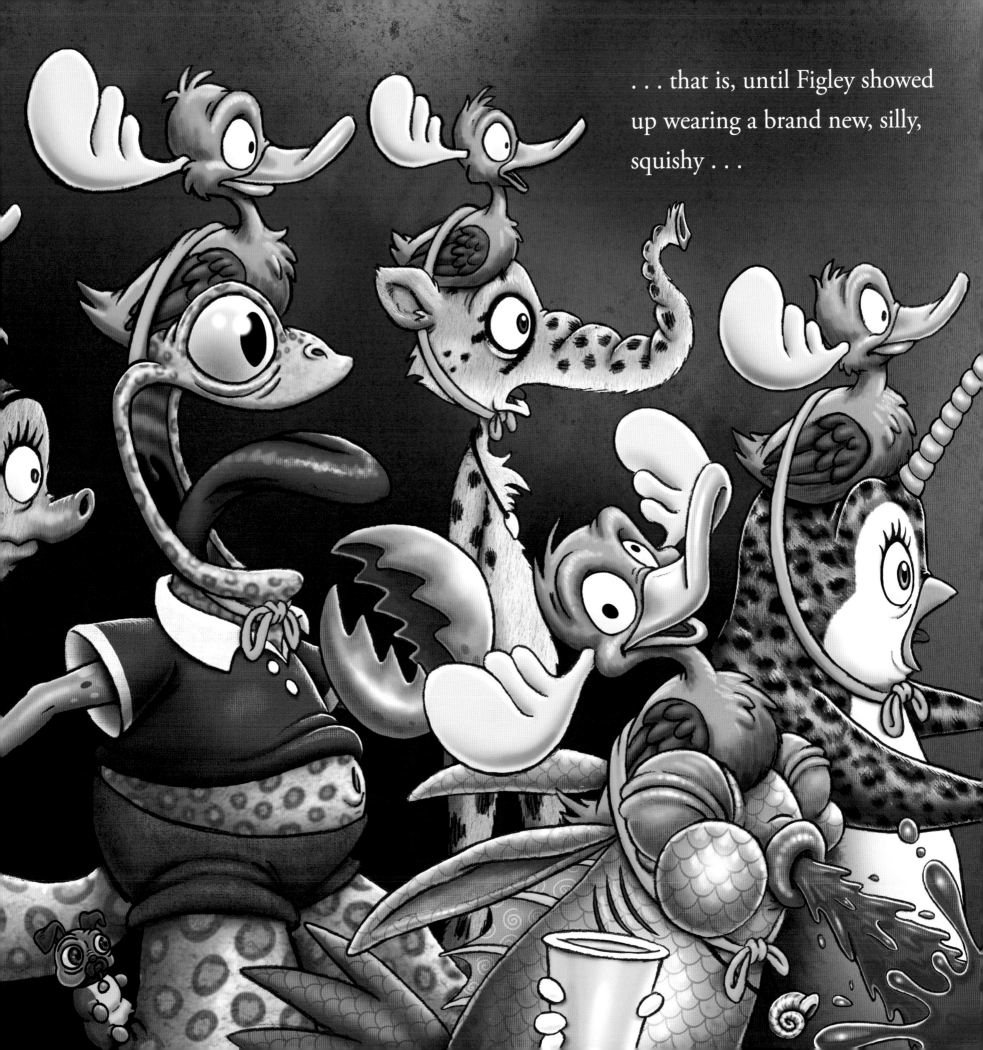

. . . that is, until Figley showed up wearing a brand new, silly, squishy . . .

SQUONK HAT!

A **squonk** is part donkey . . .

. . . and part squid.

So instead of a QUACK, his hat made a HONK!

The other kids were shocked by Figley's silly, squishy hat. It looked and sounded very different than their mookling hats.

They didn't know how to react.

But as the party went on, it was clear that in a room full of mookling hats.

. . . Figley and his squonk hat **really** stood out!

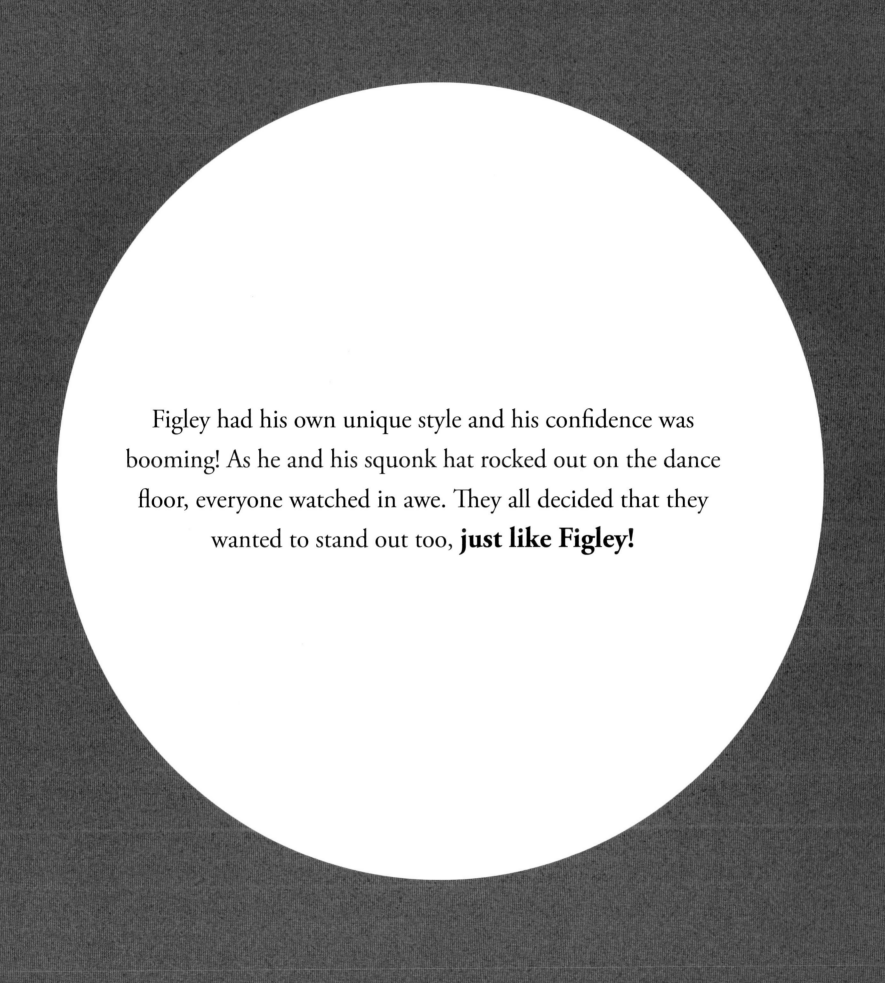

Figley had his own unique style and his confidence was booming! As he and his squonk hat rocked out on the dance floor, everyone watched in awe. They all decided that they wanted to stand out too, **just like Figley!**

The following day, Figley noticed something a little odd in the Mutropolis town square.

Everyone was wearing a squonk hat! They all wanted to stand out like Figley, but for some reason, nobody stood out. Not even Figley.

Wattee in his squonk hat . . .

. . . looked like Zabetta and Chadwick
in their squonk hats . . .

. . . who also looked like Billie
and Julio in their squonk hats.

Everyone looked the same again.

The Mutasians were disappointed. They wanted to stand out like Figley did, but wearing the squonk hats didn't seem to work.

Why?

Figley looked at his puzzled pals and explained, "If you want to stand out, don't copy me. **Mix it up!** Find something that makes you **unique**."

Be unique?

What a crazy idea!

That night when the Mutasians went to bed,
they thought about what Figley had said.

Things were about to change on the
island of Mutasia…

The next morning, Julio strolled into town with his nifty, new **nib hat**. That impressed Chadwick, who was sporting a slimy **snog hat**.

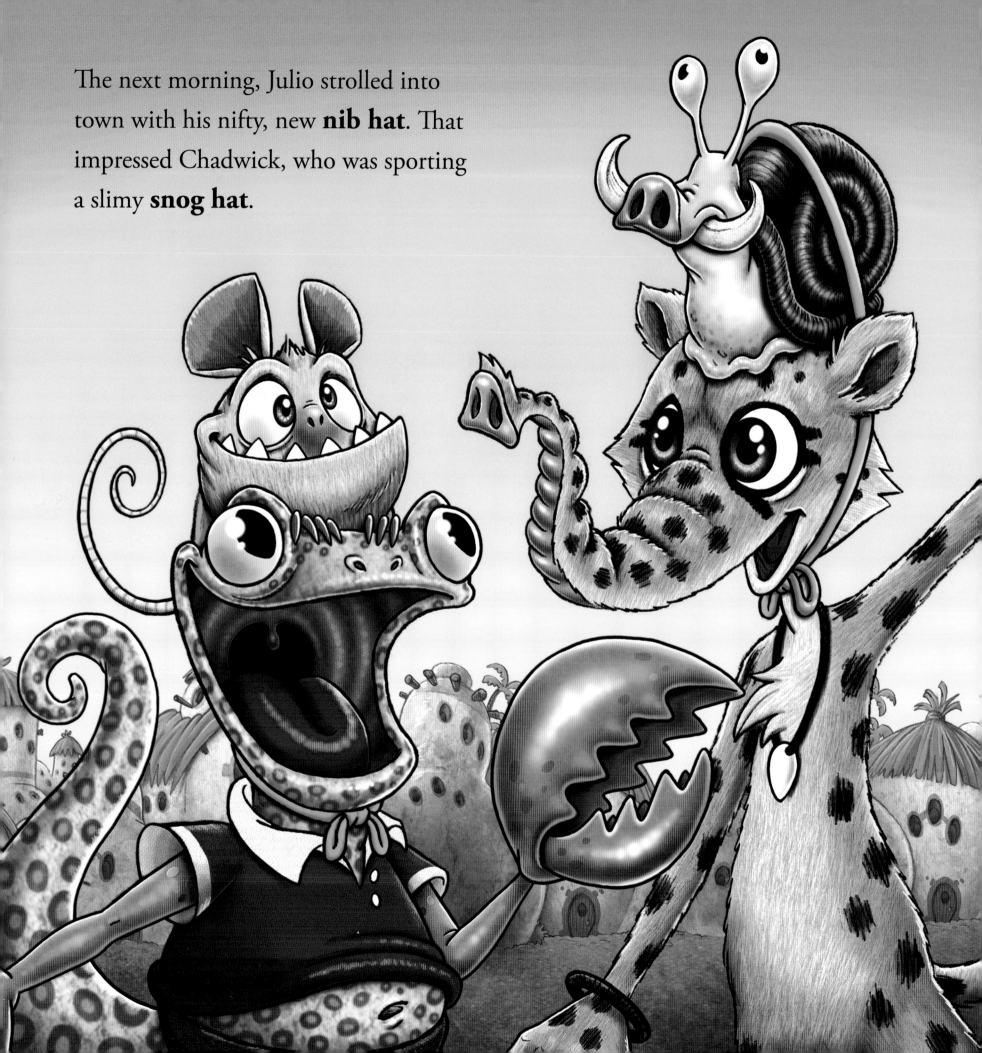

Zabetta modeled a magnificent **meowzer hat**.

She was hypnotized by Billie's hip **hissypoo hat**!

Rufus proudly posed in a prickly **pudgie hat**. Wattee, in his perfectly petite **pugapillar hat**, enjoyed a popsicle despite Rhumbler's stinky, squawking **skunkatoo hat**.

Even Flavian, the grumpy old monster who lives in a cave, expressed his individuality with a totally tasteful **turducken hat**.

Figley couldn't believe his eyes! He was in awe of the vibrant menagerie of mixed-up hats that surrounded him. The sounds of oinks, chirps, squeaks, and croaks filled the air as critters happily bounced atop his friends' heads.

Mutasia was once again full of unique individuals, and it was all thanks to Figley . . .

. . . and his **silly, squishy hat**!

THE END

Pugapillar
(pug-caterpillar)

Mookling
(duck-moose)

Julio Habañero
(gecko-crab-rhinoceros)

Billie Twinklecorn
(penguin-leopard-narwhal)

Squonk
(donkey-squid)

Queen Contessa
(toucan-giraffe)

Pudgie
(pufferfish-parakeet)

Figley
(possum-cow-finch)

Wattee
(chicken-fish-rabbit)

Winged Nib
(piranha-mouse-spider-butterfly)

Rufus
(hammerhead shark-duck)

Chadwick
(cheetah-elephant-frog)

Meowzer
(cat-lizard)

Zabetta
(pig-duck-gazelle)

Pukini
(koala-frog-rat-deer)